Dog in the Dunes

Barbara E. Cohen

**Andrews McMeel
Publishing**

Kansas City

www.andrewsmcmeel.com

98 99 00 01 TWP 10 9 8 7 6 5 4 3 2 1

ISBN: 0-8362-6920-9

ATTENTION: SCHOOLS AND BUSINESSES

Andrews McMeel books are available at quantity discounts with bulk purchase for educational, business, or sales promotional use. For information, please write to: Special Sales Department, Andrews McMeel Publishing, 4520 Main Street, Kansas City, Missouri 64111.

For Honey

Dedicated to
Aunties Mary and Marian

Introduction

I received an artist's residency from the Outer Cape Artist-in-Residence Consortium to paint in a dune shack in the dunes of Provincetown during the fall of 1996. The shacks date back as far as 1915 and have been visited by such writers and artists as e.e. cummings, Eugene O'Neill, Stanley Kunitz, Mary Oliver, Franz Kline, and Hans Hoffman.

I needed to be quiet, to paint, and to be alone . . . I needed to have my dog with me. I received special permission to take Gabe, my black Labrador, to the shack. I had intentions of continuing a series of abstract paintings that were already in progress. All that changed within the first moments of entering the dunes. Gabe was a part of that change. He followed my every step, while I unloaded supplies, cleaned the shack, and walked the beach. I was reminded that he was ten . . . he tired more quickly chasing sticks in the ocean. The days became more precious and the bond we shared deepened.

As I reviewed my work, I noticed Gabe was always searching for something . . . a stick, a treat, or maybe a ball. Compelled by Gabe, photographing his every move, brought me closer to the smells and sounds and vistas of the dunes. Sharing the isolated time and space with Gabe took me home to what I believe to be important . . . simplicity.

—Barbara Cohen
March 1998

In Memory of Gabe (1985–1997)

In the following summer of 1997, Gabe and I swam in the bay every morning side by side. I felt it was our last summer. That fall, Gabe was infected with a rare illness paralyzing him for a month. This I was unprepared for . . . a healthy retirement was my only plan. During that time, Gabe maintained his lovable and enthusiastic spirit until he was stricken with pneumonia during Thanksgiving. I lost my best buddy and a part of myself. I can still see him chasing tennis balls and searching for washed-up sea treats across the flats of Cape Cod Bay.

—B.C.

Special thanks to Louise Taylor for bringing Gabe to me and for her love and continued attempts to train him. My deepest appreciation to Mary DeAngelis and Marian Roth who helped co-parent Gabe and spoil him in all the wonderful ways aunties do. ❡ Warm thanks and gratitude to all the medical people who helped Gabe throughout his illness: Dr. Sherrilyn Brannon and Randy Caviness of Fresh Pond Animal Hospital, Dr. Stacy Sullivan of Angell Memorial Animal Hospital, Dr. Mary Rose Paradis and Dr. Kim Knowles of Tufts Veterinary Hospital, Dr. Martin Goldstein and Dr. Tina Aiken and the entire staff of Smith Ridge Veterinary Center, Dr. Katy, Dr. Randell Ferrall, and Elizabeth Herman. My deepest thanks to Dr. Joe Hyduke at Malvern Veterinary Hospital who helped carry me through Gabe's final days. ❡ For helping in their own special way, extended thanks to John Mack, Paula Gray, Pat DeGroot, Susan Seligson, Brielle Kay, Paul Churchill, Carol Ross, Chris Treibert, Sally Zeirler, Nancy Krieger, Andrea Klein, Amy Wojnar, Mariko Kamio, Maryanne Krebs, Suzy Becker, Louise Rafkin, Victoria Kapsambellis, Rose Marston, Bill Bobrowski, Tailwaggers, and the children on the East end beach of Provincetown. ❡ Many thanks again to the Outer Cape Artist-in-Residence Consortium for providing the residency at the dune shack and the support to create this body of work. ❡ Warm thanks to my parents Minna and Aaron Cohen for their generous support during Gabe's illness and to my sisters Diane and Sheila. Special thanks to David and Kerry Kay and their two children Jamie and Danny, for their constant caring of Gabe until his final moments. Endless thanks to my partner Honey Black Kay who had a secret relationship with Gabe that only the two of them knew. ❡ Last but not least, many thanks to my agents, Charlotte Sheedy and Neeti Madan, for believing in the work, and my dog-loving editors, Dorothy O'Brien, Julie Roberts, and Polly Blair, and the staff at Andrews McMeel Publishing.

—Barbara Cohen